AMBER BROWN

IS GREEN WITH ENVY

AMBER BROWN
IS GREEN WITH ENVY

Illustrated by Tony Ross

A
LITTLE APPLE
PAPERBACK

SCHOLASTIC INC.

New York   Toronto   London   Auckland   Sydney
Mexico City   New Delhi   Hong Kong   Buenos Aires

ISBN 0-439-07171-2

24 23 22 21 20 19 18 17   15 16/0

Printed in the U.S.A.   40

Interior design by Gina DiMassi. Text set in Bembo.

First Scholastic printing, August 2004

To Sarah Greene,
A Most Colorful Friend . . . .
and because she is English, she is also
A Most Colourful Friend!

Chapter One

I, Amber Brown, have had enough. "Dylan Marshall, you are driving me crazy."

Dylan looks at me and smiles. Then he pretends to be guiding a steering wheel. "Vrroooooom. Vrooooooooom. Zoom."

His older sister, Polly, looks up from the book she is reading. "Dylan, you are so immature."

"Thank you." He bows to her.

She sighs and goes back to her book.

Before my dad rented the downstairs half of their house, I used to think that Dylan was one of the BIG kids, a sixth grader.

Now I think that he's just a BIG doofus.

Dylan pretends to drive into his younger sister, Savannah.

She ignores him.

"Road pizza," he yells, pretending to run over their cat, Mewkiss Membrain.

"I'm going downstairs," I announce.

"You're supposed to stay up here until THE DADS come back from getting the groceries," Polly reminds me.

I sit down and look at a magazine, thinking about how my life has changed in the last few months.

THE DADS . . . my dad and their dad . . . if grown-ups can be best friends, I think that's what they are becoming.

My dad was not happy when he moved back from France.

I, Amber Brown, think that he wanted to get back with my mom, but it's too late . . . she's going to marry Max.

Dylan comes over and makes an armpit noise at me. "I'm bored."

"You're boring." I smile at him.

"Thank you." He makes a bow.

Actually, I, Amber Brown, think that Dylan can be fun. But not today.

Today he is driving me crazy.

I'm staying at my father's house for Christmas vacation. So my mom went to California to visit her sister, my aunt Pam. Dad wants me to call his house "our house," but sometimes I forget because it doesn't feel like our house yet. Actually, I spent Christmas Day and one day after that with Mom at her house, which I do think of as my house because I've lived there all my life.

I, Amber Brown, have two houses because I, Amber Brown, am a shared-custody kid.

It's a little weird to live in two houses, especially since they are very different from each other.

In the house where I live with my mom, it's just me and Mom. Max visits a lot. It's going to be a little weird when they get married, but since it's only December and they're not getting married until June, I'm not going to think much about it now.

In this house, my dad rents the basement

and first floor of the Marshalls' house. There are four Marshalls who live upstairs. . . . . The dad, Steve . . . . . Polly, who is in high school . . . . . Dylan and Savannah. Inside the house, we don't keep the doors locked between the two places, so it's almost like we are all living together. In fact, the dads got a sign for the front door that reads:

I hope that Dad stays here. He's made so many changes . . . . when he left our house, when he left the country, when he came back.

He promised me that he's not going to leave again.

He didn't promise me, though, that he would stay here forever.

It's not always easy being a shared-custody kid.

Dylan looks under the Christmas tree. "Where did I put my new computer game?"

He keeps searching, picks up a package and throws it to Savannah. "Catch."

It hits her on the foot.

"Ow." She glares at him.

It's the present that I gave her, a soap-making kit called Gross Soap.

"Amber," she says, "let's make soap today."

I was hoping that she would make the soap soon, but my dad said that I should wait to see what she wanted to do, because it was her present . . . . . not mine.

I really wanted it for me, but my dad said that I had enough presents already. I gave it to Savannah so that maybe I could make the gross soap anyway.

"There's nothing else to do. So this is your lucky day. I'm going to make soap too," Dylan says. "But first, I am going to get a snack."

He leaves the room.

Polly looks up from her book. "Does anyone in this room want to play a joke on Dylan?"

Savannah and I raise our hands.

Chapter
Two

Savannah and I go over and sit on the couch
in front of Polly.

She smiles at us. "That boy is driving me
crazy."

"Me too," Savannah and I, Amber Brown,
say at exactly the same time.

We link pinkies.

Polly says, "We have to talk quickly before Dylan gets back. Here's what's going
to happen. I'm going to tell a joke that makes
absolutely no sense . . . . . no sense at all . . .
but when I get to the punch line, which is
'No soap. Radio,' you two are going to

laugh a lot, and so will I. That will confuse Dylan."

I like that!

Savannah says, "I don't get it."

"Exactly," Polly explains. "The joke doesn't make any sense. Dylan will see us laugh and feel stupid that he doesn't get it. Or he will laugh, and then he'll feel stupid when we make fun of him for laughing at a joke that makes no sense."

She whispers, "When he hears the three of us laughing, he's going to think that he's missing something, and that will bother him. He's such a know-it-all."

We all smile at each other.

"Amber, when he comes in, tell a short joke. That way it will look like that's what we've been doing while he was gone." Polly looks at the doorway to see if he's on his way. "Okay, now."

Dylan rushes in. "I made popcorn, but it's just for me."

Sitting down, he shoves a huge handful of it in his mouth and goes, "Yum."

At least I think it's "Yum," because with the wad of popcorn in his mouth and the wet pieces spraying out, I'm not sure of the exact word.

I turn back to Savannah and Polly.

"What's the longest word in the English language?" I ask, and then yell out loudly, "Smiles! Because there is a MILE between each S . . . . sMILEs."

"I EW AT." More popcorn falls out of his mouth.

"I have a great joke." Polly leans forward.

Savannah and I pretend to be excited.

She leans down. "Two polar bears are sitting in a bathtub. The first one says, 'Pass the soap.' The second one says, 'No soap. Radio.' "

Immediately Savannah and I look at each other and laugh . . . . . and laugh . . . . . and laugh.

I start rolling around on the floor. "No soap. Radio."

Savannah rolls also. "No soap. Radio. That is so funny."

Polly says, "It's the best joke I've heard in years."

I sneak a look at Dylan.

He's stopped guzzling popcorn into his mouth.

He looks confused.

Polly looks at him and then talks to him in that older-sister voice. "Dylan. Don't you get it?"

He just looks at her.

She looks at him. "Dylan. Two polar bears. Bathtub. No soap. Radio. Savannah and

Amber are younger than you . . . . . and they
get it."

I roll around some more. "No soap. Radio."

I sit up and try to catch my breath. "Dylan.
Do you want me to explain it to you?"

"No." He looks annoyed. "You don't have
to. I get it. I just had too much popcorn in

my mouth before. I get it. It's very funny. No soap. Radio."

He laughs in a phony way.

Polly, Savannah and I look at each other, clap our hands and laugh even more.

"Sucker," Savannah yells. "We fooled you. Fool. Fool. Fool."

Dylan looks at Savannah.

Dylan looks at me.

Then he looks at Polly and says, "What's so funny?"

"You are." She smiles at him. "We got you. That really wasn't a joke. We pretended it was, and you believed us."

"Funny. Funny. Funny." Savannah rolls around the floor again.

"Noooooooooooo soap. Radio," I tease.

"Girls," he yells. "I hate girls. It was bad enough when I just had my two sisters here . . . . . and now, you too, Amber Brown. It's like I have three sisters. Ugh. Yug. Barf."

He stomps out of the room.

We sit there quietly for a minute.

"There's nothing to do," Savannah says. "That was fun. Now I'm bored."

"Maybe we should turn on some music," Polly says.

I shake my head. "No radio. Soap."

It is time to make soap.

I just hope that Dylan doesn't do something to get even.

Chapter
Three

We're in the kitchen. It's Soap-Making Time.

I wonder if the pioneers made soap the same way we will be making it.

We've got everything out . . . . . the Gross Soap kit, the molds and extra supplies that my dad and Steve bought for Savannah.

Polly reads the instructions. "This looks simple enough. First melt the wax in a container."

I, Amber Brown, hold up a plastic measuring cup. "Container ready."

Polly continues. "Once it's melted in the microwave, the wax is to go into the molds."

"Molds." Savannah holds up some of the plastic molds.

"Choose objects to put into the hot wax once it is in the molds."

"Gross stuff." Savannah and I both hold up some of the creepy crawly things that came with the kit.

She's got a worm and a spider in her hands.

I've got a beetle and a cockroach in mine.

I'm glad that they are plastic.

Polly laughs. "I'm putting in some of the other things that the dads bought." She picks up a little rubber ducky and a mini mermaid.

Somehow I don't think that the pioneers made soap the way that we are.

I don't think that they had microwaves in their cabins.

The phone rings. Polly rushes over to pick it up.

I hope that it is Brenda, who is her best friend and my Ambersitter.

It's not.

I can tell because Polly listens for a minute and then hangs up the phone without saying a word.

She shakes her head. "It's Dylan, trying to disguise his voice. He just asked if our refrigerator is running and if it is, he thinks that it's running down the street."

The phone rings again.

Polly answers it again.

Again, she says nothing and just listens.

Finally she says, "Yes . . . . I have seen a lamb chop, but not at a karate exhibit. . . . No, I have not seen salad dressing . . . . and trying on new clothes. . . . Dylan, would you just stop calling? If you want to make soap, come in now... and stop being such a Goofbrain."

"Doofus," I say. "He's a Doofus Goofbrain."

She hangs up and looks at us. "I'm going downstairs. I bet he's using the phone in your house, Amber."

Polly leaves the kitchen.

The phone rings again.

I look at Savannah, who sighs.

I make a face and pick it up. "That's enough, you Doofusbrain. I don't want you calling here anymore."

I stop to hear what Dylan has to say for himself.

"Amber? What's going on there?" It's my mother's voice.

Ooooooooops.

"Hi, Mom," I say. "Are you having fun with Aunt Pam in California?"

"Yes," she says, "a wonderful time. . . . BUT . . . have you been getting bad calls?"

She sounds worried.

"No, Mom," I tell her. "Dylan's just been calling and telling dumb jokes . . . . and he's driving us crazy."

"Using your phone?" she asks.

I nod.

"Using your phone?" she repeats. "I tried calling there, but the line is busy."

I guess she didn't hear my nod.

"I guess," I say. "Polly's gone downstairs to check."

My mom knows about how it is here at "The Zoo."

One day, she brought me over to Dad's house.

She said that she just did it because she

was running some errands in that neighborhood and it would save him the trip to pick me up.

I know that she just did it so that she could check out what my other house was like.

My dad knew too, I think, because he gave her a tour of the two places and introduced her to everyone.

Now I think that she feels a little better about me being at Dad's house. I mean Dad's and my house.

And she knows that it is okay to call the Marshalls' number if no one answers Dad's phone.

"I just called to say hello," she says. "I miss you lots."

"So you are having a wonderful time at Aunt Pam's?" I ask.

"I am," she says. "Tomorrow we are going to Disneyland. I really wish that you could be with us . . . . . but I know that you are having fun with your dad."

My mom. My aunt Pam. Disneyland. California.

I feel bad that I am not there.

I miss her.

I miss seeing Max.

I wonder if he is missing her.

I wonder if he is missing me.

"Amber," Mom says, "I'll be back in a few days and then you'll be back home on New Year's Day. I can't wait to see you."

"I can't wait to see you either," I say.

It's weird. I didn't think about missing my mom until she called.

I haven't felt too bad about her being in California and me staying in New Jersey . . . until now.

Chapter Four

I, Amber Brown, am now one unhappy Amber Brown. How dare they go to Disneyland without me?

I don't think that's fair.

I don't think it's fair that Mom told me that they were going without me.

If I weren't a shared-custody kid, I would be there right now with them.

I'd be going to Disneyland.

Dylan comes into the room, playing the accordion that his uncle Hugo sent him.

The Marshalls' uncle Hugo is always sending Dylan very loud instruments as presents.

Steve says that his brother does that for all of the years of teasing that Steve did to Hugo when they were kids.

I think about how Mom and Aunt Pam are in California and will be going to Disneyland and hanging out with Mickey Mouse and Goofy . . . . . and how I'm here in New Jersey and hanging out with Dylan, who is acting very Mickey Mouse and Goofy . . . . with an accordion.

I, Amber Brown, am green with envy.

That's what my parents say means "very jealous."

Well, I, Amber Brown, am green with envy.

I am not only green. . . . . I am feeling blue. . . . . I am seeing red. . . . . I am purple with anger. . . . . I am not feeling like a rainbow. I am feeling plaid. All of these colors mix together to make a not very pretty pattern.

I, Amber Brown, do not like plaid.

And I don't think my mom should have called and made me feel so bad.

I look at Dylan, who is now playing the accordion while balancing a can of soda on his head.

I want to cry.

My dad and Steve walk into the room, carrying bags of groceries.

Steve looks at Dylan, takes the can of soda off his head and says, "Dylan, my son, let's call Uncle Hugo, and you can play a song for him on that fine accordion. And if he is not in, you can play every song you know onto his answering machine. I won't mind paying for that phone bill."

"Amber," my dad says, coming over and

giving me a kiss on the top of my head. "We're going to have dinner up here with Steve and the kids tonight."

"Mom and Aunt Pam are going to Disneyland tomorrow," I tell him.

My dad says nothing for a minute and then he sighs. "Did your mom send you a postcard and tell you that?"

"No," I say. "She called. She misses me."

My dad sounds a little angry. "And she doesn't think that I miss you when you are with her? But I don't call you up and tell you that."

I look at him. "Yes, you do."

He starts to say something, but doesn't.

Then he says, "Amber in the Middle."

I look at him again. "That makes it sound like a game . . . . . but it's not a fun one."

"I know," he says.

Polly comes back into the kitchen. "I just heard the accordion recital that Dylan is leaving for Uncle Hugo on his answering machine. Our uncle is going to be very happy that the delete button was invented."

That makes me laugh, but I kind of wish that Polly hadn't come in just now. I wish that Dad and I could have talked more about "Amber in the Middle" and how I feel about that. It's kind of hard, though, to ask her to leave since this is really her kitchen. And it's kind of hard for Dad and me to leave because it would seem rude.

Steve and Dylan come back into the room.

Dylan is still playing the accordion.

I wish that someone had given him lessons for Christmas.

I wish that his uncle had given him a CD with good accordion music on it.

I'm not sure that I would like accordion music even if it was played well.

My dad takes out his wallet. "Dylan. Five bucks, just this one time, if you play far, far away every time I ask you to."

"I don't know that song." Dylan stops squeezing on the accordion.

"It's not a song that I'm talking about," my dad teases. "It's distance. . . . I don't want you to PLAY a song called 'Far, Far Away.' I want you to GO far, far away to play."

I, Amber Brown, know that my dad is kidding around . . . but I hope that doesn't make Dylan feel bad.

Dylan doesn't, because he turns to everyone and says, "Anyone else willing to make the same deal? Five bucks so that I don't play the accordion around you."

His dad gives him five. I give him one. (Dylan said that I get a junior citizen discount.) Savannah gives him fifty cents. Polly gives him a dollar and fifty cents.

Dylan counts it up. "Thirteen bucks. My first gig. Maybe I can organize a concert that I promise not to play at. . . . . . I could make a lot of money that way."

Dylan leaves with his accordion.

Something tells me that this is the best dollar that I have ever spent.

Soon we are all together again and ready to make soap.

When the liquid soap comes out of the microwave, we pour it into molds, pick out the dyes that we want to add to it, color the wax, and then put things in it.

I make mine light red and put the cockroach in it.

It looks really gross.

I, Amber Brown, really love it.

My dad makes one and puts a tiny tennis racket in it.

I make one for him. It's got a make-believe cell phone in it. That's to remind him to stay off the cell phone when we do things.

It used to make my mom really mad that he was on the cell phone all the time.

My mom . . . . . I remember . . . . this time tomorrow she will be in Disneyland.

Sad.

I'm not sure what kind of soap I should make her.

I decide to use the heart mold, put pink soap in it and then add red glitter.

I decide on that because I love my mom, but also because sometimes I feel like a heart soap that gets goopy/melty after it's used.

Polly yells, "Dylan! I hate you."

I look over at Dylan and Polly. Polly looks really angry, really angry . . . . . and almost ready to cry. She is staring at the table in front of them.

I look down.

She has a lot of Polly Pocket toys, old ones and new ones, little ones and big ones. She doesn't play with them now that she's a big kid. She collects them because of her name.

Dylan's taken Ice Castle Polly, Vet Polly, Slumber Party Polly and Mermaid Polly and put them into the hardening soap. The heart, circle, shell and star cases are sitting there without their Pollys.

Steve goes up and looks closely at what Dylan has done.

Dylan gets sent to his room.

We try to rescue the Pollys, putting them under hot water to melt the soap.

The Pollys are freed, a little cleaner . . . all except for Ice Castle Polly, who has gone down the drain.

The Pollys are no longer in hot water.

Dylan still is.

He has to give Polly the thirteen dollars that he just got . . . . . and seven dollars more.

We continue to make soap.

I make one for Max. I put some miniature bowling pins and a tiny bowling ball in his soap cake. Max is the coach of my bowling team.

My dad looks at it and I can hear him mumble, "I hope that guy strikes out."

I, Amber Brown, am a little confused. People get strikes in bowling and that's a good thing. People strike out in baseball and that's a bad thing.

My dad knows sports, and I don't think he's confused about strikes in baseball and bowling.

I think that he's talking about splits, how Max and Mom should break up.

It's a bad thing when my dad does that.

And I don't like it when my mom says bad things about my dad either. She does that sometimes, especially after she has talked to him on the phone.

Sometimes it feels like a sports game and that I, Amber Brown, HAVE to choose one team over the other.

Chapter
Five

Packing.

I, Amber Brown, am packing to go back to the house where I live with my mom.

Into my suitcase go the clothes that I brought over.

Into my knapsack go my schoolbooks with the homework that I did over the holiday.

It will be great to see Mom.

I will miss being with Dad and with the Marshalls, but it will be so wonderful to see her and to have some quiet time again . . .

time where Dylan won't be around, driving me crazy!

I wonder if Max will be there when I get back. I wonder if he missed Mom almost as much as I did.

I look around the room.

Dad and I went shopping for things to decorate, and I got some great stuff.

On my wall is a large neon clock. It not only keeps time, but if I don't turn it off, it's like a giant night-light.

I also got a purple Lava lamp, which Dad and I named Lana the Lovely Lava Lamp.

In my closet are a whole bunch of new clothes, ones that will stay here. Dad says that I won't have to cart a lot of stuff back and forth. But I know that he really wants my new stuff to stay at this house. I wrote little D's (for Dad's house) on the labels so that I remember what stays in this house.

When I get to Mom's and my house, I'll write M on the clothes that stay there.

I look at my clothes once more before I go.

It was so much fun to shop for them.

Polly and Brenda went with me to choose things at the stores where I had gift certificates, the stores that already had after-the-holiday sales.

Dylan said that to do as much shopping as we did, for so many hours, would have been the worst torture for him.

I loved shopping with Polly and Brenda.

After it was all finished, we went to the

food court and looked at boys' rear ends and decided which were the cutest.

I, Amber Brown, felt like I was a teenager like Polly and Brenda even though I really don't care about boys' rears.

I look in my top dresser drawer . . . . . panties, which I really needed, a bra, which I really don't need, some socks (glittery), a set of gloves, mittens and a scarf (all purple).

In the next drawer are four pairs of the black pants that I love to wear. (I know what I like!) . . . . . Also two T-shirts and four long-sleeve shirts.

Also a fuchsia sweater, a pink sweatshirt, two purple tops, three nightgowns and one pair of pajamas (with the feet and the trap-door back!).

Dylan may think that shopping is awful . . . but I think that it should be an Olympic event.

I look at my new watch.

The other one that I have, the one that

I used to love so much and be so proud of . . . when I got it in the second grade . . . seems kind of baby now. . . . It is in my jewelry box. I bought one like the one that Polly has . . . . . black and silver with little rhinestones in it. I think that it's okay to wear the same watch at both houses. . . . I don't know what the rules are on that one.

I wish I had a divorce rules book, but I still haven't found one.

"Amber, honey," my dad says, knocking on the door. "Almost ready? Your mother said that she wants you back at the house by four o'clock. And you know that when your mother wants something, she gets cranky when she doesn't get it . . . . . and we don't want that to happen, do we?"

I don't know what happened when my dad spoke to my mom, but he sure got into a terrible mood.

I, Amber Brown, think that he is getting very cranky, and it's making me nervous.

I had such a good time until now, when I have to leave.

My dad puts the luggage into the trunk of the car, and we drive to my other house.

Dad hasn't said anything since we got into the car.

I try to make things nice. "Dad, I had a really good time. I'll be back for a visit soon."

That doesn't make things nice.

He makes a face. "It's not just a visit," he says. "You live with me too."

I don't know what to say.

I don't know why I said "visit."

I wish that my father wasn't acting like this. He was so much fun over the whole vacation.

We get to my mom's and my house.

My dad takes the luggage out of the trunk and says, "Amber, honey . . . . . I'm sorry that I am in this lousy mood. I just hate to see you go . . . . and I don't like to be bossed around by your mother."

As far as I can figure out, all that my mom said was that I had to be home by four because she and Max and I had dinner reservations at six, and she wanted me to get settled first.

Now my dad is in a totally awful mood.

"Dad," I say, "I can take my luggage in myself."

He just looks at me. "All of this?"

"I can make a couple of trips," I say.

My dad picks up the bags. "They are too heavy, honey. I don't mind carrying them . . . . . anything for my girl, who, by the way, I am going to miss very much."

"Me too," I say. "I'm going to miss you."

It's true. I will miss him, but I really do want to see Mom and Max right now. I just don't want to let him know that and have him feel really bad.

The front door opens.

"Amber," my mom says, holding out her arms for me.

We hug, and then Max hugs me.

My dad steps up and then walks to the door. "Where do you want me to put these?"

Max answers, "You can just leave them inside the door."

My dad nods and walks inside with the luggage.

As he goes in, a piece of luggage sort of hits Max's leg a little.

It looks like Max is going to say something, but then he doesn't.

My mom says, "Phil, while you are here, would you like to come in and we can talk about Amber's schedule for the next few weeks? We have some plans that need to be worked out."

"I have some plans too," my dad says.

Max puts his arm around my mom's waist and says, "I'll go get some soda for everyone. I know what everyone else likes, but what should I get for you, Phil?"

"My usual, a root beer," my dad tells him.

"We don't have root beers in the house anymore," my mom says.

My dad shakes his head. "You still have water, yes?"

She nods.

I, Amber Brown, am feeling very uncomfortable.

Max returns with the drinks and sits down on the couch next to Mom.

I wish that they hadn't asked my dad to come into the house now.

My dad looks around the room. "What ever happened to that picture that my mother gave us for our wedding?"

"It's in the attic," my mother says. "I put it there with a lot of other things."

I remember the day that she went all over the house, taking things down, packing things up and putting them in the attic.

My dad looks at a beautiful bowl that is on the table. It's a brownish color and written on it is the word AMBER. "I remember the day that I bought that bowl for you. It was the day that Amber was born."

My mom smiles for a minute.

Then my dad looks around the room and starts naming other things that he gave Mom or that they bought together.

He accidentally spills some of his water on the table and stands up. "I'll clean it up.

Is the towel rack in the same place it always was? Remember how much trouble I had getting that on the wall?"

My mom looks uncomfortable.

Max looks uncomfortable.

I feel uncomfortable.

I wish that my dad would leave soon.

My mom looks at Max. "I'll go talk to Philip in the kitchen for a minute and work out the schedule."

When she leaves, Max says, "Amber, you are going to love the souvenirs that we brought back for you from Disneyland."

WE . . . . . WE . . . . . I think.

"I thought Mom went alone," I say quietly. "I thought you were here, in New Jersey, in your apartment."

Max makes a face. "Oh, right. . . . . . Well, I missed your mom so much that I went out to California and stayed in a hotel while your mom stayed at Aunt Pam's."

Somehow it really doesn't seem fair that Max and Mom got to go to Disneyland. Somehow, I wish that I had known that Max was there so I wouldn't have wasted my time worrying about him missing Mom.

My dad and mom come back into the living room.

They don't look very happy.

"Time for me to go, honey," my dad says to me. "I'm going to miss you."

We hug.

As he leaves, he turns to Max and says, "If there's ever a problem with anything in the house, just give me a call. I know how everything works here and I'll be glad to show you how to fix it."

Mom and Max don't look happy when he says that.

Somehow, I don't think that they are going to be asking for his help.

After Dad has gone, I look at Max and Mom, who are looking at each other. They look angry. I know that they are not saying anything in front of me.

Max carries the bags up to my room, and I get dressed for the restaurant.

Max and Mom talk downstairs.

When we get to the restaurant, I sit down to hear their news.

It can't be that they are getting married. I already know that.

Mom looks at me very seriously. "Amber, Max and I have already talked about this at great length. I realize that you may have some feelings about this . . . . . but we want to let you know that we are not going to stay in THAT house. We are going to move."

Move. We can't move. We just can't move. I've lived in THAT house for my whole entire life.

My mom continues, "We want to be in a house where we can have people come to OUR house, Max's and my house . . . and your house. Where Max and I and you can create our own history."

I feel like I've been hit by a ton of wet noodles, mixed in cement sauce.

"When? Where?" I want to know.

"When? Soon," Mom says. "Where? We don't know."

"In the same town?" My voice is getting a little louder.

Mom shrugs. "We don't know yet."

I don't want to move to another house, to another town.

I want to stay right where I am.

I don't know what to do, what to feel, what to say.

For once in my life, I, Amber Brown, am speechless.

Chapter
Six

January 11.

I'm back in school.

Life as I know it is over.

Mom and Max weren't kidding.

We are really going to move. They are already looking at houses. When they find a house or houses they like, they will show them to me, and I can help them decide. I like that they want me to help them decide. I, Amber Brown, got very mad at my dad when he picked a house without me. Now Mom and Max are letting me decide . . . except for one thing. I have decided . . . I want to stay exactly where I am. I like my room. I like knowing exactly where everything is. I like my friends. I like knowing my neighborhood.

Mom and Max said that once we find the house and buy it, they are going to get married. They aren't going to wait until June. We will all move into the house at the same time.

They won't promise me that we will stay in the same town.

That means that I may not even stay in the same school.

I, Amber Brown, always feel bad for kids who have to move and go to a new school, especially in the middle of the year.

I remember how bad I felt for Justin, my best friend who had to move.

Mrs. Holt is in the front of the classroom, taking attendance.

I really like Mrs. Holt.

I like all of the teachers at my school . . .
I've had some great teachers here. . . . . Mrs.
Holt . . . . Mr. Cohen . . . . Ms. Light. . . .

What if there are no great teachers at my
new school?

What if they never smile at me? What if
they already have favorite students, and there
is no more room in their brains to add another favorite? What if they have already
memorized all of their students' names, and
they have no more room in their memory for
mine? What if they think of me as "What's-
her-face, that new kid who came to the
school in the middle of fourth grade?". . . .
What if everyone thinks that it is weird for
me to say, "I, Amber Brown"?

There are so many more what-ifs.

What if my dad keeps getting madder
and madder about this?

When I was at Dad's house, I should never
have told him that Mom and I and Max were

going to move. He got on the phone to Mom and yelled and yelled and yelled. He said that he had moved back to this town, not to New York City, because of me, so that we could spend time together . . . . . and how dare they think that they could move. He used the words "I'm calling my lawyer." He used them a lot.

I'm not sure, but I don't think he should have acted the way that he did when he dropped me off at the house after Christmas vacation . . . . . talking about how he knew where everything was, and how he had been a big part of the house for a long time.

My dad. I'm just getting used to shared custody, to living in both houses. If I am living in another town, what if he decides to move to New York City? That will mean that I won't see him as much, and I won't see the Marshalls as much . . . . . and Brenda won't be my Ambersitter anymore. And

Mrs. Holt won't be my teacher. There will be a lot of won'ts.

I've never really been mad at my mom before, not like this . . . not BIG TIME. . . . I may even hate her. . . . I may even hate Max. (If it wasn't for him, none of this would happen.) Why did he and Mom fall in love? Why did I start to care about him? And my dad isn't acting great either. I could hate him too. I know that it is bad to hate . . . but I can't help it.

Mrs. Holt has a few students pass around some paper. My friend Brandi is one of them.

"Amber." Brandi hands a paper to me and leans down and whispers, "Are you okay? Why are you crying?"

I didn't even know that I was crying.

I put my head down on the desk.

She leaves and a few minutes later, Mrs. Holt comes up to my desk. "Amber, would you please step outside with me for a minute."

As we leave, she says to the class, "All right, everyone. I want you to start your writing assignment now . . . . . and I don't want to hear a sound out of anyone."

I stand outside the door with Mrs. Holt.

I, Amber Brown, am even upset with Mrs. Holt. Why does she have to be such a good teacher that I am going to miss her?

"Do you want to tell me what is bothering you?" Mrs. Holt takes out a tissue and wipes my eyes.

She's being so nice . . . . that makes me cry even more.

I tell her what is happening.

Every once in a while, she has to stick her head back inside the classroom to remind the class to quiet down.

The class . . . . . I will miss them too. Fredrich and his nose-picking fingers . . . . Brandi . . . . . Kelly . . . . . Alicia . . . . . Tiffany and her collection of Barbie dolls . . . . . her little brother, who is always committing Barbiecide on the dolls . . . Bobby . . . . . everyone . . . . everyone except for Hannah Burton.

"Amber." Mrs. Holt leans down.

"Yes." I sniffle.

"Are you sure that your mom is going to buy a house that is not in town, that you will have to leave the school?" she asks.

I shake my head no. "But they may. They said that they might buy a house someplace else."

"Have you told your mom how upset you are?"

I shake my head no again.

Mr. Robinson, the principal, comes by.

Mrs. Holt says that she wants to talk with him for a minute.

They go stand about ten feet from me.

I just stand where I am, sniffling.

They come back, and Mrs. Holt says, "Amber, honey. Would you like to go sit in Mr. Robinson's office until you feel better?"

I sniffle more. "Am I in trouble?"

I, Amber Brown, have never been inside the principal's office. I thought that was only for bad kids.

Mr. Robinson leans down and says softly, "No, Amber. Not at all. I promise. We just want you to calm down, to be able to talk about what is bothering you."

All of a sudden, what is bothering me is that I'm not sure that I want to talk with him about what is bothering me. I'm also not sure that I can go back into the classroom again. I don't want everyone to see me cry, especially not Hannah Burton.

I'm not sure what I want to do.

A lot of kids say that it is really scary to go to the principal's office.

I've never heard anyone say, "I'm going to the principal's office, goody!"

We all just stand there.

The class starts getting a little noisy again.

Mr. Robinson just walks to the door and looks in.

The class gets quiet, fast.

Mr. Robinson comes back again.

I, Amber Brown, have to make a decision, and I have to make it now.

If I go back into the class, I'm afraid that I will start crying.

If I go to Mr. Robinson's office, I may start crying too . . . . . but at least there, I know that he is not going to call me a baby for crying . . . . . and I know that Hannah Burton is.

I, Amber Brown, am going to the principal's office.

Chapter Seven

The principal's office . . . . . everything looks so serious.

He has one of the biggest desks I've ever seen and he's got one of those big chairs that a person can twirl around in.

I just can't imagine Mr. Robinson twirling around and around in his chair.

There are pictures of his family on his desk.

It looks like he has two kids and a wife and two dogs. I never thought that a principal would have a child with a nose ring (the girl) and a child with an earring and turquoise hair (the boy).

It looks like their family is still together, a happy family.

I bet the Robinson kids never had to move.

I bet that their parents never got divorced.

I sigh . . . . . a very loud sigh.

"Amber." Mr. Robinson leans forward. "Would you like to talk with me about what is bothering you?"

Looking at him, across the desk, I shake my head no and then start talking.

My head is saying no, but my mouth talks anyway.

First, I tell him about my parents separating,

and my dad moving away . . . . . and my mom crying a lot in the beginning . . . . and my dad moving to Paris . . . . . and then coming back . . . . . and how Mom met and is going to marry Max . . . and that I don't know who to choose . . . Max or Dad . . . and how I was doing badly in Mrs. Holt's class, not turning in homework or anything . . . and how I'm doing well now . . . . . and how now my mom is going to sell the house and how we are going to have to move . . . and maybe move out of town . . . and I'm going to have to leave the school . . . . and why should I even bother to do well if they don't even care about what I want?

I am losing control . . . . . and I don't think that I am ever going to calm down.

Mr. Robinson just sits there listening.

I cry really hard. There are tears coming out of my eyes, gunk coming out of my nose.

The tissue that Mrs. Holt gave me is soaked.

I throw it in the wastepaper basket.

It misses.

Looking up at Mr. Robinson, I wait for him to yell at me and make me stay after school.

I pick the wet tissue up again and drop it into the wastepaper basket.

This time it goes in.

Mr. Robinson hands me a box of tissues.

I hope that I don't use them all up.

Blowing my nose, I say, "Thanks."

He smiles at me. "Amber . . . . . I'm going to let you in on a secret. I have a little re-frigerator hidden in this office."

He walks to a closet door and opens it up. "What kind of soda would you like?"

I sniffle and then grin at him. "Do you have crème soda? That's my favorite."

"Mine too," he says.

I can't believe it . . . . . the principal of my school likes my favorite soda.

He hands me the soda and then goes into

a drawer and brings out several different kinds of Twizzlers, black licorice and chocolate and strawberry.

"Amber," he says, "we'll talk about what is bothering you, but first I'm going to show you something that makes me smile when I am upset. First, though, I have to ask . . . you are not allergic to any of this and you are not a diabetic . . . . and your parents let you eat candy?"

I nod and giggle. "My dad lets me eat more candy than my mom does."

He says, "Okay . . . . . then here goes. Which Twizzler do you think will go better with crème soda?"

I shrug.

I've never thought about that before.

He hands me one of each, and then gives himself a chocolate one.

He bites off each end of his Twizzler and uses it as a straw. "Yummmmmmmmmmm."

I giggle and try all three with my soda.

The chocolate Twizzler straw with crème soda is definitely the best. The strawberry one is okay . . . . . the black licorice one is a little pukey.

I smile at Mr. Robinson.

It's the first time I've had a real big happy smile since Mom and Max told me that we would have to move.

We talk more about how I am feeling.

Mr. Robinson says, "I'll give your mom a call tonight and let her know what we've talked about, if that's all right with you."

I nod.

"I want you to know," he says, "that this may not change what is going to happen. There are times in our lives when we have to do things that we don't like. . . . Nothing's perfect, life doesn't always seem fair. If you have to move to another town, go to another school, it may be hard for you . . . but I think you are a terrific kid, and you'll do all right. And you can always write to me . . . . . and I'll write back."

I really like Mr. Robinson.

That makes me want to cry again.

I'm sorry that I really like him so much.

That's one more person that I'm going to miss.

Chapter
Eight

I'm back in class.

I have washed my face, and I hope I can hide the fact that I've been crying.

What I can't hide is the fact that I have been eating black licorice. I know this because when I went into the bathroom to wash my face, I stuck my tongue out at myself, and my tongue is black.

I look at the board.

Birthdays:
1775—Alexander Hamilton—first U.S. Treasury secretary
1885—Alice Paul—founder of the National Women's Party and women's rights leader
1938—F. E. Moulton—the first American woman to become a bank president
Events:
1878—Alexander Campbell became the first milkman to deliver milk in glass bottles.
1935—Amelia Earhart was the first woman to fly solo across the Pacific—her 18-hour flight went from Honolulu to Oakland.

*1964—The Surgeon General declared
cigarettes hazardous to health!*

Other Special Events for January 11:

*This is International
Thank You Day
&
A Special Day that you will
find out about later!!!!!*

Ever since we came back from vacation, Mrs. Holt has been putting the day's list of happenings on the board.

I am very happy about that because for Christmas I gave her a book of events throughout the year.

I even have the same book at my house. I gave that to myself as a Christmas present.

Mrs. Holt asks us what interests us about the list.

Bobby Clifford says, "I thought only girls are secretaries. How come Alexander Hamilton was a secretary, and he's a guy?"

Alicia Sanchez raises her hand and turns to Bobby. "Doofus."

"No name-calling," Mrs. Holt says.

Alicia stares at Bobby. "Men can be secretaries too. It's a good thing that Alice Paul was born to help women's rights. . . . It's a shame that she isn't around to help you, Bobby."

She says "Bobby" in a tone of voice that sounds like she is saying "Doofus."

Fredrich Allen raises his hand. "Being a secretary in the United States Cabinet is different from the traditional secretary."

For a nose-picker, Fredrich Allen is very smart.

Bobby shakes his head. "I don't get it. Why was Alexander Hamilton in a cabinet? Didn't he have a room?"

For a non-nose-picker, Bobby Clifford is not very smart.

Mrs. Holt looks at Bobby as if she is not sure if he really can't figure it out or if he is just being stupid.

She explains what the President's Cabinet is.

Brandi waves her hand.

Mrs. Holt calls on her.

"I'm glad that the Surgeon General said that cigarettes are hazardous to our health. I wish that my grandpa had listened. He didn't, and he got lung cancer."

She looks sad.

I feel bad for her.

I am glad that the grown-ups in my life do not smoke, even if I am so mad at them.

Next we talk about whether we get milk delivered or whether we get it from the store. Everyone says that their milk is from the store. No one knew that milk was ever delivered to houses.

Jimmy says that when he was little, he got milk from his mother.

"Gross," Hannah Burton says.

Mrs. Holt says, "It's really not gross."

Hannah makes a face and looks disgusted.

I stick out my licorice-covered tongue at her.

She looks at it and again says, "Gross."

This time she is talking about my tongue.

Mrs. Holt says, "I'm going to read to you all now. . . . This is a wonderful book."

She holds up a picture book.

"That's baby," one of the boys says. "That's for little kids. We read chapter books now."

Mrs. Holt smiles at him. "It's never baby to read a good book."

We all wait to hear the book and decide for ourselves.

Because it is Amelia Earhart's birthday, Mrs. Holt reads *Amelia and Eleanor Go for a*

Ride by Pam Muñoz Ryan. She also shows us the illustrations. I wish that I could draw like Brian Selznick.

After she is done, we all decide that a good book is a good book.

Mrs. Holt says, "Class . . . . now we have a special surprise!"

She goes over to the intercom phone and picks it up. "Hello. This is Mrs. Holt. Would you please ask my friends to come to our class now?"

She puts down the phone, and we all wait to find out who the friends are.

The people walk in.

Some of the kids yell out, "Mom."

That's because their moms have walked in.

Their moms are the room mothers.

Mine isn't because she has to work.

I'm glad she isn't because I definitely don't want to see her now.

The moms just stand there while Mrs. Holt says to us, "Listen carefully. . . . Today is 'a fruit comes apart' day. Can you think of another way to express that? If someone in this room can, we can celebrate."

I think about it . . . . a fruit comes apart.

Vinnie yells, "Apple turnover."

Mrs. Holt shakes her head no.

Everyone is quiet, trying to think about it.

I keep saying a fruit comes apart . . . a fruit comes apart . . . a fruit comes apart . . .

"Blueberry crumble." Hannah sounds very proud of herself.

"Very good," Mrs. Holt says, "but in this case, not correct."

Hannah looks crumbled.

Again, I say to myself, "A fruit comes apart." And then I figure it out.

"Banana splits!" I yell.

Mrs. Holt smiles and then goes over to the board and writes out:

January 11 is
Banana Split Day!

73

"Hooray for Amber." Brandi claps her hands.

I smile at my friend.

The moms set up a table with banana split ingredients.

We all go over to the table and tell them what we want.

I get to go first because I guessed.

My day is getting better.

I wish that every day could be Banana Split Day.

When we are all finished, the room gets cleaned up, and we all sit down again.

The moms go out of the room.

We all wave good-bye and smile at them.

Then Mrs. Holt writes our homework assignment on the board.

Since today is International Thank You Day, write a thank-you letter to someone you know. Bring it in tomorrow.

This assignment does not make me happy.

Who am I going to write to? . . . . . Not my mom, not my dad, not Max. . . . . There's nothing that I want to thank them for, not today.

I think about writing to Mrs. Holt, but I bet a lot of people are going to write to her.

I make my decision.

I'm going to write a thank-you note to Mr. Robinson . . . . . to thank him for listening to me, for teaching me how to make a Twizzler straw and for saying that he is going to talk to Mom.

I am thankful that there is someone that I want to write a thank-you note to.

Chapter
Nine

Kelly Green and Brandi Colwin come up to me after school. "Amber, are you all right?"

I nod my head yes and then I shake my head no.

They are my two best friends in the whole school, in the whole town, in the whole state of New Jersey.

They can't be my two best friends in the country or in the world . . . . because of Justin Daniels, who is my best friend who moved away in third grade, all the way to Alabama.

Justin is my best friend in Alabama. In fact, he is my only friend in Alabama. I miss his mom and his dad and his little brother, but they are not my best friends.

Anyway, I have three best friends and Kelly and Brandi are the ones who I see all the time. They are the best friends who like to talk on the phone, who like to put on nail polish with me, who I can really talk about my feelings with. Justin is not good at those things . . . . but he is very good at having fun and at making me laugh and for knowing me for my entire life.

I think about it.

I, Amber Brown, have three best friends and all of them have moved. Justin moved away in third grade. Kelly moved here this year, in October. Brandi moved here in third grade, and we became friends in fourth.

Moved . . . . . there's that word again.

M O V E . . . . . that's a really bad four-letter word.

I hate that word.

I, Amber Brown, hate the word H A T E
. . . . . another bad four-letter word.

They are both words that I am saying a
lot . . . . . . and will have to say more.

"Brandi. Kelly," I say. "I hate to tell you
this . . . but I may have to move. Mom and
Max are looking for a new house . . . . . and
it may not be in town."

Brandi and Kelly practically fall to the
floor.

They both start to cry.

That makes me start to cry.

"Listen." I sniffle. "I've told you. Now I
can't talk about it anymore. It makes me too
sad."

"Amber," Kelly says, "should I call my
mom and ask if you can come over? Then
you won't have to stay in Elementary Ex-
tension."

I don't think that I could stand being in
that room today, where everyone just sits

around or does something just waiting for someone to pick them up.

I nod.

Kelly goes into her backpack and takes out her mobile phone, a Christmas present from her parents.

Kelly Green has a mobile phone, parents who are still married to each other, and she has no problems.

I, Amber Brown, am green with envy about my friend Kelly Green.

That makes Kelly a green without envy.

She is so lucky.

And she has a sheepdog too, named Darth Vader . . . . . a dog that doesn't even mind when we put nail polish on his toes. She

has a cat, Fluffy . . . who doesn't let us polish her toes.

I can't have animals because my mom is
allergic to them.

I hope that wherever we move once had
a kennel of dogs and cats living in the house,
and the animal hair is still all over the place,
even in the paint in the walls. That will give
my mother something to sneeze at.

Brandi sighs. "Amber, I am so sorry that
I can't come over too. But I have a music
lesson and my parents said that if I don't
go to my lessons, I have to pay out of my
allowance for the ones I miss . . . unless I'm
sick . . . . . and there is no way that I can
say that I am sick and then go over to Kelly's
house."

Brandi says, "I'll call you tonight. Gotta
go now."

Kelly talks into the phone for a minute
and then smiles, turns off the call and puts
the phone into her backpack. "Mom said

it's fine for you to come over to the house. She's going to call your mom to make sure that it is okay with her . . . . . and then your mom will call the school and let them know that it is okay."

Mrs. Green and Max are the two grown-ups, other than my parents, who can take me out of school . . . . . and my parents have it worked out that when one of them takes me out of school for something, then the other one has to give permission.

Not all of the kids in school have to have both parents' permissions, but some do. I think it's a divorce thing.

I know that neither of my parents would kidnap me. I know that's why there is the sign-up thing. They don't think that kids can figure that out, but we can. My parents would never do that . . . . . unless moving counts as kidnapping.

Kelly and I wait for her mom in front of the office.

"Ms. Brown. Ms. Green." Mrs. Parker, one of the fifth-grade teachers, comes up to us. "Aren't you two quite the colorful pair! Brown and Green. It sounds like a meeting of Boy Scouts and Girl Scouts."

Today, I am not in the mood to hear colorful jokes.

I wonder if I said something to Mrs. Parker about her name, how she would feel about that.

I think what I could say . . . . . like "If you are a twin, does that make you a double-parker?"

Mrs. Green arrives before I say anything.

That's probably a good thing.

I, Amber Brown, am getting grumpy . . . and that's not a good thing.

The way that I'm feeling now is not like me.

I'm really mad, and I can't seem to get out of my mood.

I've never been this mad . . . . . not even

when my dad left our house and moved into an apartment . . . . . not even when my dad moved to Paris.

I was more confused and hurt then. Also, I was worried about how my mom felt, and I thought that it was my job to take care of her.

This is different.

Taking a deep breath, I try to figure things out.

I'm not confused. . . . I know what is happening. My parents are very angry with each other. Max, who I've never seen angry, is angry at my dad. My dad is angry with Mom and Max. Sometimes they get angry at me because I am not thinking or doing things the way that they each want. I am angry at my parents and Max.

I'm hurt . . . . but not like I was when my parents broke up. I don't think that anything can ever hurt as much as that.

I don't want to take care of anybody . . .

not my mom . . . . not my dad . . . . not Max. I want them to take care of me. After all, I am the kid.

Kelly and I get into her mom's van.

I, Amber Brown, have noticed that most families have vans. Mom and I don't because there are only the two of us. Mom always calls vans "the taxis of the suburbs." Even with Max, I don't think that we are going to need a van. Only big families with animals need vans. Three people don't need that much room. We don't have cats. We don't have dogs. We don't have lots of children, just me . . . . . and that is more than enough for a regular car. I like our car.

The van is full.

Darth Vader is in the very back of the van in his cage. He doesn't like being in his cage, but if he's not, he jumps around the car, licking everything and slobbering. Lick and slobber. Slobber and lick. People.

Upholstery. Windows. He's one very odd lick-and-slobber dog.

The groceries are in the backseat section.

Kelly's baby brother and little sister are in the seats behind the driver's seat.

The kitchen sink is on the seat next to Mrs. Green.

Actually, I, Amber Brown, am just kidding.

It's not the sink . . . . . just a new faucet for the kitchen sink.

We get into the section with the groceries.

Kelly's little sister and brother are in the seats in front of us.

Linda, who is three, is singing *Sesame Street* songs to her Barney.

I just don't like that dinosaur, even if he is my favorite color, purple.

Joey is asleep. Little bits of spit are coming out of his tiny mouth. He must be getting lessons from Darth Vader. At least he doesn't lick, at least not yet.

We get to Kelly's house and help unload the car.

Mrs. Green looks tired.

Linda wants to show us how she and Barney can dance together.

Joey starts crying.

Before I remember how angry I am at

my mom, I think about how nice and quiet it is in our house.

Then I remember how angry I am at my mom, and I don't care to think of anything nice about her and the house that we are going to leave.

Linda opens a box of cereal that Mrs. Green has just unpacked.

Before we can stop her, she has shredded the box and there is cereal all over the kitchen floor.

She really murdered that box of Alpha-Bits.

That makes Linda a cereal killer.

I laugh so much when I think of that . . . "cereal killer," serial killer. Sometimes I really crack myself up.

We help clean it up, and then go to Kelly's room to do our homework.

I write my thank-you note to Mr. Robin-son.

Kelly keeps writing her thank-you note.

She won't tell me who it is for.

I look at her bookshelf while she is finishing up.

Kelly has such good books . . . . . we share our books.

Kelly finishes.

"Amber Marie Brown," she says, "I want you to read this."

She hands it to me.

It's her homework assignment, her thank-you note.

Dear Amber,

I want to thank you for being so nice when I moved here.

I was so scared and unhappy.

Saying good-bye to all my friends in Metuchen was so hard. I was afraid that they would all forget about me, and no one here would want to be my friend.

I hated moving into a brand-new house and leaving my old one.

All morning before my first day of school, I cried.

The only person that I was going to know in class was Hal, because he lives next door, and I'd only just met him.

I begged my parents to let me stay home for the day, for the week, for the rest of the school year, but no, they made me go.

And then I got there and Hannah Burton was the first kid in the class to talk to me. And she didn't seem *nice, even though she tried to act nice.*

It was so good when you got to school, even though you were late.

I, Amber Brown, remember that day. I'd overslept. My teeth weren't brushed. My hair wasn't combed.

Hannah was mean to me.

And then Mrs. Holt asked me to show Kelly Green around. At first, I was a little bit upset that someone else had a colorful name.

I continue reading Kelly's letter.

Then you showed me around the school, and we talked, and you didn't even make fun of me when I barfed all over myself.

I also remember that . . . . . it was Ping-Pong Barf.

I made a stop at the nurse's office with Kelly, and we saw this little boy throw up.

Kelly threw up when she saw the kid lose his cookies . . . and then he threw up again and then she lost hers again. It was not great to look at . . . . . or to smell.

Then when I came back to school after getting cleaned up, you were very nice.
(Even though you did tell the boys and they sang "Happy Barfday" to me.)
And you share your friends with me.
You don't get annoyed when Brandi and I do things without you.

Actually, that's not quite true. I got very upset when they went to the mall without me and got their ears pierced . . . . . even though it wasn't their fault . . . they asked me to go but my mom said no.

Anyway, I just want you to know that you are a really nice person (funny, smart, caring, kind) and I want you to stay here. If you can't stay, I'll be really sad, but I know that wherever you go, people will think you are wonderful.

I know that it's not easy to move and that parents get to make all of the decisions, but you are going to be all right.

I want to thank you for being a good friend.

Your pal,

Kelly Green

I reread the letter.

It makes me want to cry.

It also makes me want to smile.

It makes me feel better about being able to take care of myself, no matter what happens.

My dad left, and I survived.

Justin left, and I survived.

And if I have to move, and if my parents keep on fighting, I'll survive . . . . . and I'll

do it Amber Brown style . . . . and that's
okay.

I know that now . . . . . and I only hope
that I don't forget it.

Chapter
Ten

"Amber, we have to talk," my mother says.

I just stare at her and don't say anything.

"Amber, we have to talk," she repeats. "We really have to talk."

I continue to stare at her.

My mother stares back.

She blinks first.

I win.

Somehow it doesn't feel like I'm winning anything great by staring my mother down . . . . . but I'm still glad that I did.

She sighs.

I finally blink, but blinking after a sigh is not giving in.

She sighs again.

It looks like she's going to cry, but then she just gets an upset look on her face. "Amber Brown. Your attitude is not helping the situation."

"This situation is not helping my attitude." I, Amber Brown, am surprised that I say this, but I'm glad that I have.

What is she going to do, send me to my room?

I don't care. I like my room, and since I'm going to have to move away from it, then I might as well spend as much time in it as I can.

I go to the refrigerator and take out the container of orange juice.

Pouring it into a glass, I concentrate on not spilling any.

"Amber." My mother speaks softly. "I know that you are angry. I understand *why* you are so angry."

I put down the orange juice container and finally speak. "Do you really?"

"I think so." She nods. "And Mr. Robinson talked to me about what you told him."

Good for Mr. Robinson, I think. I wonder if he would adopt me.

I think about being Mr. Robinson's kid … a life of Twizzlers and soda. I do remember, though, that some kids think that he can be really strict sometimes . . . . . and I'm not sure it would be fun to be the principal's kid.

I stare at my mother, trying to look really mad, but feeling like I want to cry. "I really don't like what you are doing . . . . moving us . . . . . and deciding to move without talking to me about it first."

My mother nods. "Honey, I think that Max and I owe you an apology."

"We're not moving?!" I clap my hands.

My mother pours herself a cup of coffee and then says, "Honey, let's sit down and talk this out."

I think about it . . . . . will sitting down and talking about the move mean that I'm going to give in . . . . . and they can move me out of my house, out of my town? Will I be able to convince them to leave things just the way they are?

I sit down and take a sip of orange juice.

She smiles, sits down and takes a sip of coffee.

I take another sip of my orange juice.

She takes another sip of her coffee.

First we had a staring contest . . . . now we seem to be having a "sipathon."

Finally, my mother speaks. "Max and I have been talking about moving for a long time. We want to live in a larger space. We want more room."

"You know," I say, blinking back tears, "when my father left, you started asking me a lot of questions about what to do. You let me help make decisions. When I was littler, that was hard for me. Now I'm used to helping make decisions. Now that you and Max are getting married, is it back to the way it was when you and Dad made all of the decisions? . . . . . Only now it will be you and Max making all of the decisions?"

She just looks at me, really thinking about

what I have said. "Oh, Amber. I didn't realize that I was putting all that responsibility on you. I'm sorry."

"Well, you did," I say, "and now you are just going to take it all away. I don't think that's fair."

"Amber, don't you want to relax and just be a kid again?"

"Too late," I say. "You can't just take all of that away . . . . and anyway, it's not fair for you to just move a person without her permission or discussion."

She thinks about it and then nods. "I understand. From now on, Max and I will talk with you about life-concerning decisions involving you."

"Good," I say.

Mom continues. "But the reality is that we must move . . . . for the reasons we've already discussed. And we definitely need more room."

"Why?" I ask.

She explains. "There are many reasons. We need a guest room so that there is room to put people without having them sleep on a living room sofa. Don't you think that Aunt Pam would like that?"

"I can let Aunt Pam take my room, and I'll sleep on the sofa. I've done that before," I tell her.

Mom shakes her head. "What about when Max's sister and his niece come for a visit?"

"I can sleep in the backyard," I say. "I can put up a tent."

"If they visit in the winter?"

"I can stay at Brandi's or Kelly's." I smile at her. "Please. Oh, please. Don't make us move."

"Honey," she says, shaking her head.

I have noticed that my mom calls me "honey" when she wants to tell me something that I don't want to hear.

"It's not just the guest room. We need more room so that Max and I can have office space. And we need more room because sometime you may have a baby brother or sister."

Shocked. I am shocked. I put my head down on the table and say nothing for a minute.

If my mother thought that this talk was going to make me less upset, she was wrong.

Raising my head, I say, "Baby? Who said that we were going to have a baby?"

Then I ask a question that I never thought I would ask my mother, my own mother. "Are you getting married early because you are going to have a baby soon?"

She gasps. "Amber. How could you have thought that?"

Why do parents always think that kids never think about or can figure out some things easier than the parents thought they could? I watch television. I listen to people in supermarkets talk. I even heard my dad talk to Steve about the wedding date change, and they wondered if Mom was going to have a baby soon. I don't tell my mom about that, though.

I do say, "Mom, I thought that you and Max were going to involve me in any decision-making that has to do with me? This definitely affects me."

She laughs and then stops when she sees that I don't see anything funny. "Amber, this is really something that is between grown-ups . . . . between Max and me."

"But it affects me. There will be another person, a fourth person in the family," I say.

"The decision to have a baby is one that adults make," she says firmly. "Amber, you used to say that you wanted a baby brother or sister."

"That's when you and Dad were married," I say. "Now it's you and Max."

I can tell that she is trying to talk her way out of this.

She says, "Amber. We're not talking about having a baby immediately. We want to get used to living together, Max and I . . . . . you, me and Max . . . . a baby may come later. . . . Just think . . . . . someday, your own baby brother or sister!"

"Baby half brother . . . . . or half sister. We'll have different fathers," I remind her.

She smiles. "Half brother . . . . half sister. Does that really matter?" she asks. "Amber Marie, they are going to be part of our family . . . . all family. Half brother. Half sister. What's the other half going to be?"

I think about it and decide to joke. "Tuna fish . . . . half tuna fish."

I try to think about what a half baby—half *tuna fish* would look like.

Thinking about it makes me laugh. I think that the words tuna fish are funny. I don't know why.

"Okay," I say. "We can have a half tuna fish—half human baby . . . . but that's it."

Sometimes it's easier to joke about something serious than to really deal with it.

As long as they aren't planning to have a baby for a while, I feel better. Maybe they will change their minds.

Mom continues to explain why they want and need more room. In addition to wanting more room, they want to live in a house that my dad never lived in . . . . that they didn't want him to walk into their house and act like HE was the one who once lived there, who had rights because of that.

"Amber," she says, "you can understand. Can't you?"

I think about the way my dad acted when he brought me back to the house.

He shouldn't have acted that way.

He just doesn't get it . . . . . he and Mom are not going to get back together again.

Sometimes I wonder why they broke up. I used to think that I was the reason they broke up, but now I don't think so. I've given up trying to guess. They won't tell me.

Even I, their kid, don't think that they should get back together...well, mostly I don't think that they should get back together.

I do want to suggest one more thing. "Why don't we just leave things the way that they are? Max in his apartment? We can stay in our house?"

She shakes her head. "That won't work. Max and I really want to live together in *our* own home."

"Yours and Max's?" I ask.

"OURS," she says. "Mine and Max's and yours."

"If I say that I understand why you want to leave the house, can you understand why I hate it, and why I want to stay in the same town?"

She nods. "Understanding, though, doesn't mean that we won't move to another town . . . . we still may . . . . but . . . . . I promise that we will try to stay in the same town. That's fair to you. . . . . . That's fair to your father too, I guess."

I ask her another question that I really want her to answer. "Do you hate Daddy?"

"No," she says. "I don't hate him . . . . but I definitely do not want to remarry him. I love Max . . . I want to marry Max . . . . . and I don't want your father to dictate where or how Max and I will live."

It is not easy for me to figure all of this

out . . . . but this move is because of my dad . . . . so he is dictating it.

I say, "Mom, please promise me that you will try to find a house in town."

She nods. "We will *try*."

She said that so quickly.

I wish that I hadn't used the word TRY and asked her to promise that they WOULD find a house in town.

Somehow, I don't think that she would have made that promise.

I guess that I'm just going to have to wait to find out.

Chapter Eleven

My dad has a date.

He's going out with some lady he met today at the grocery store.

Most parents leave grocery stores with bags filled with food and toilet paper.

My dad leaves with the telephone number of the woman he met in the freezer section while deciding which flavor of Ben & Jerry's ice cream to buy.

She suggested Chubby Hubby.

Then she said that, as a single person, it was the only hubby in her home.

I should have gone with him when he

asked me to go instead of taking a bath.

I would have told him to buy the chocolate chip cookie dough.

But I wasn't there, so he got Chubby Hubby ice cream and a date for tonight.

He promised to take me to the movies tonight.

Now he is taking a stranger to the movies instead.

He promised to take me.

I think about it.

When he was looking for apartments, he promised me that I could help him choose one . . . . . and then he found this place without me.

After that, he said that he would NEVER break a promise to me again . . . . and NOW he has.

I'm sitting in this house, very mad.

I'd call Mom and go home, but I know that she and Max have gone to New York City to a play.

My dad keeps saying that he really wants to spend some time with me, especially now that there is a chance that I will be moving to another town.

So here I am at his place, and there he is, out on a date with someone who he just met today at the Grand Union.

I am not very happy about it.

In fact, I am VERY NOT HAPPY about that. My dad keeps saying how upset he will be if I move away. He keeps saying that he is going to get a lawyer to make sure that I don't move out of town . . . . that he will spend as much time and money legally as it takes to spend time with me.

And then he leaves.

On a date with someone he doesn't even know.

I am not only not happy. I am very sad. I am very angry.

I'm here at his house, without him.

Steve is also not here.

He's gone to a party.

Savannah is also not here.

She's gone to a friend's pajama party.

I could have gone to Kelly's house. Brandi's there tonight. We could have had a pajama party too.

Dylan is here, in his room playing computer games.

I am not alone, though.

Brenda, Polly and I are giving each other facials.

I'm hanging out with the teenagers.

If I weren't so angry with my dad, I would be having a totally great time.

Now it's only a sort of great time because I'm feeling sad and mad.

"Leave it on for twenty minutes and be careful not to get any of it in our eyes." Polly looks up from reading the instructions. "Also, maybe we shouldn't put it on our lips. We don't want to swallow it."

Soon our faces are totally green.

We've got scarves so that the gunk does not get into our hair.

It's really nice of Polly to share the Christmas present that she got from Brenda.

The green gunk hardens on our faces.

We can't really talk.

We can't even smile.

Dylan walks into the kitchen and looks at us.

He pretends to be terrified. "Oh, no. It's the creatures from the Green Latrine."

Dylan starts talking to himself. "Okay. I won't let them get me. I know there is a way to save myself. Let me think. With vampires, it's garlic. With the creatures from the Green Latrine, it's . . . . . !"

He goes to the freezer, pulls out an ice cream sandwich, goes back and takes two more. "Now I'm safe."

Polly makes a face. The gunk cracks and flakes. "That boy will find any excuse to eat as many ice cream sandwiches as he can."

We go to the sink and wash the mess off our faces. Then we put this clear smelly stuff on and then the moisturizer.

I look in the mirror.

My face looks exactly the same except for the green face mask still in my eyebrows.

We all look at ourselves in the mirror for a while and then start playing Go Fish.

It's a lot of fun spending time with Brenda and Polly.

Sometimes I wonder if they would be hanging out with me if it weren't for the Ambersitting money. . .but then there *are* other times that they do just hang out with me.

Brenda's boyfriend had to go with his family to Pennsylvania, to visit his grand-mother.

Polly doesn't have a boyfriend.

Neither do I.

I don't want one.

I think that Polly does want one.

She keeps mentioning a boy named Lenny, who is in her political science class. Brenda and Polly keep calling it "poli sci." Then they joke that Polly sighs over Lenny in that class.

I hope that I never get that silly over boys when I am a teenager.

I decide to change the subject. "I need to ask you something."

We stop playing Go Fish.

I ask, "Do you think that you are part of a normal family? Do you know normal families?"

Both of them laugh.

It's not a mean laugh, though.

They are not laughing at me.

"Describe normal," Brenda says.

I shrug. "I don't know . . . . . parents who aren't divorced . . . . . kids who don't feel bad sometimes . . . . . people who things go well for . . . . . normal."

"I've heard rumors that there really are normal families," Brenda says, and smiles.

"Yes. We're discussing them in poli sci." Polly giggles. "Look, Amber . . . . . there are families that are intact, not divorced, not separated, that are considered normal. Talk to any of them . . . . . and you'll see . . . . they have problems too."

"I think that the biggest problem is that people think that just a few things are normal . . . . and that's not true," Brenda says. "People judge too easily."

"Do you think that the only families that are normal are the ones who are married, never divorced, perfect?" Polly asks.

Thinking about it, I sort of nod.

"Sometime you should ask the kids in those families if they think that their families are normal. I bet that some of them will say yes . . . . . and some of them will say no," Brenda says.

I look at Brenda, who has dyed her hair green and red for the Christmas holidays. She also has dyed some of the tips of her hair blue and silver for Hanukkah. Some of the tips are also black to go with the green and red for Kwanzaa.

I'm not sure that Brenda is an expert on normal.

"There is no such thing as normal," Polly says. "Look at my family. . . . a lot of people at school who don't know me look at me and think I come from a normal family. And I'm sure that if they knew us, they wouldn't call us normal . . . . but our life is normal to us. . . . . . My dad is here . . . . my mom went to South America with some other guy . . . . . is that normal?"

I, Amber Brown, never knew that.

"Are they divorced?" I ask.

Polly shakes her head no. "My mom doesn't answer any of her mail, and she doesn't contact us."

I stop thinking about what is normal and think about what is going on in their family.

"Do you miss her?" I remember how I used to miss my father when he was in Paris . . . . but he always kept in touch.

Polly shakes her head no and then yes. "I do . . . . but mostly I am mad at her . . . . especially when I hear Savannah cry . . . . or Dylan cry."

I think about how hard that must be.

I'm a little surprised to think about Dylan crying.

I'm not surprised about Savannah.

Polly continues. "I have had to take care of my brother and sister much more than I would have had to if my mom was around. I love them, but sometimes it would have been nice to be able to be a kid who didn't have to act like an adult so much of the time."

"Poor Polly," I say.

She smiles at me. "It's not easy, but it's the way it is around here . . . . and not all of it is bad. I'm a lot less spoiled than some of the people I know. I just worry about how everyone is going to manage when I go away to college in two years."

I didn't know all of this about the Marshalls . . . . wow . . . . . no wonder Steve looks so tired some of the time . . . . . and so does Polly.

Polly looks at me. "So now you know . . . my family would not be considered normal either . . . . but it's the family I know, and I love them . . . . well, all of them except for my mother."

Brenda says, "And I think that my family is normal . . . . what's left of it. . . . . My dad died, so there is just my mom and me . . . . but that's still a family.

"I've thought about this a lot," Brenda continues. "At school, there are kids who are adopted, kids who were born into the family where they are living, kids who have stepfamilies, kids who have two mothers, kids who have two fathers, kids who live with guardians . . . . . so many different ways to live . . . . . and who gets to decide what's normal?"

"It bugs me when one group tries to decide what's normal for everyone." Polly shakes her head. "That causes problems everywhere . . . . in school, in the country, in the world. Fights and wars can start that way."

"The way I figure it," Brenda says, "as long as it doesn't hurt yourself or others, then it's fine."

We all smile at each other.

Then we go back to playing Go Fish.

Polly and Brenda start discussing the butts

of boys in their classes . . . . . rating them from asinine to buttacious.

I decide that it's time to go.

This may be normal behavior for them, but I'd rather go read a book.

Chapter
Twelve

My mother puts the bowl of cereal on the table in front of me. "Honey, be outside right after school. Max and I will be there to pick you up."

I pour milk into the bowl.

I'm the one who has to do it because I know just the right amount to pour.

If I put in too much, then it gets soggy. I hate soggy cereal.

If I put in too little, then it's dry.

Then I have to add more milk, and then there's leftover milk, and I have to add more cereal.

I stir the mixture.

"Amber," my mom says, looking at me, "did you hear what I said?"

I nod. "Be in front as soon as school is over. You and Max will be there to pick me up."

She moves closer to me, putting her face right in front of mine. "And you do know why we are picking you up, right?"

I pick up the spoon of cereal and try to put it in my mouth.

Some milk dribbles down on both of us.

My mom backs up and sighs. "Amber. Why are we picking you up? Why have I taken several days off from work?"

It's my turn to sigh. "You and Max are looking for a new house . . . . . and I have to go to school."

She nods. "You can't miss school. Even if your grades were better, I still wouldn't take you out of school for this. But we want you to be part of the decision-making, so we are narrowing down the choices . . . . . and now there are some that we want you to see."

I look around the kitchen. Under one of the cabinets is a plaster of paris mold of my handprint that I made in preschool with a nose print in the middle made by Justin.

 Miss Emily, our teacher, had to clean the plaster of paris out of his nose before it got hard.

By the stove are pot holders that I made in first grade. I never could get all of those loops closed off correctly, but Mom said that they were beautiful anyway.

On the wall is the corkboard that I made at day camp. We tack things on it, like appointment reminders, pictures and coupons.

I wonder if we will put up all of these things in our new kitchen when we find the house.

I wonder if I hate the houses, will they buy one of them anyway. . . just saying that my opinion matters but not meaning it.

The doorbell rings.

It's Max.

He's driving me to school today.

We go out to the car.

On the front seat is a wrapped present.

I get into the car and put my seat belt on.

The present is between us.

Max starts up the car and says, "Amber, the present is for you."

Christmas is over.

It's not my birthday.

"Is this a bribe?" I ask. "So that I'm not mad about having to move?"

Max smiles and thinks about it.

Then he nods. "Sort of . . . . but it's also an I-love-you present . . . an 'I'm glad that you are going to be my daughter' present . . . and 'I'm glad that we are all going to be living together' present."

I think about it. "But I already have a dad . . . . you are going to be my stepdad."

Max nods again. "I know. But I want you to know that I feel like you are my daughter . . . . . and that no matter how many children your mom and I have . . . . you will always be my first daughter . . . . and that doesn't mean that I need to have you love me more than Philip, your real dad."

I don't say anything.

He continues. "I know that you are very angry at your father right now . . . . . but he is your dad and he does love you. . . . I just want you to know that you don't have to choose between us . . . . . that we can both be important to you."

I can feel tears in my eyes. "You are very important to me."

Max smiles. "Good. Now open your present."

I rip the package open.

I, Amber Brown, am not good at opening packages slowly.

I open the box lid.

There's a ceramic plaque that reads AMBER BROWN'S ROOM.

I smile at Max.

"Your mom and I went to one of those ceramic-painting places and we made this for you. I did the printing. Your mom did the painting."

I look at the plaque. There are pictures of things that are important to me. The pig alarm clock that Aunt Pam gave me . . . cartoon pictures of me, Mom and Max . . . also a rainbow and crayons.

"I love this." I smile again.

We are stopped at a traffic light, and Max looks at me. "We've decided to paint a set of plates for the new house."

"You and Mom?" I ask.

He nods. "And you too. Once we get settled, we'll do it. I'm not very good at this, but it's something your mom really wants to do . . . . . and"—he grins—"you know when your mom really wants to do something . . ."

I finish his sentence. "She gets it done."

We both grin.

The light changes, and we continue on to the school.

When I get there, Max parks, gets out of the car and opens my door for me.

He makes a big deal of my getting out of the car, sort of like I'm a queen or a princess.

I leave the present in the car.

I don't want it to break at school.

We hug each other good-bye.

"See you after school," he says. "With any luck, we'll find a wonderful house that we all like."

I cross my fingers.

We hug again.

"Bye," we say, and then I skip up over to the playground.

One of the playground aides says, "That was very nice of your dad to open the door for you and to treat you like such a lady."

I open my mouth to explain that Max is not my dad . . . . that he's not even my step-dad yet . . . . and then I close my mouth and just nod.

I wonder what it's going to be like at Parents' Night.

Chapter
Thirteen

Dear Justin,

I know that my mom and your mom have been talking on the phone a lot lately.

How do you like having a new baby sister? I think it's funny that Danny asked if they could take it back to the store and exchange it for a baby brother . . . or even better, a GI Joe action figure. (Someday, I will probably want to talk with you about baby brothers and sisters, but not yet. . . . . . Now I want to talk to you about moving.)

I know that our moms talk on the phone a lot . . . . and that your mom knows what's happening here.

Because you had to move away, I have to ask your advice. (I can't ask Kelly and Brandi . . . . because they don't want me to move away . . . . . and they will pick the house in town.)

Please let me know what you think. (I know that you don't like to talk a lot about feelings, but please do this for me!!!! Please, oh, please.)

I know that it was hard for you to move away, that you didn't want to talk about it . . . . . but was it hard for you when you got to Alabama? Did you miss being here? Do you still sometimes miss being here even though you've been gone for over half a year? If you could still live here, would you?

I wrote myself a note about the houses and I want you to look at it. Writing it

all down is helping me figure things out.
After you read my notes, please call. . . .
Please, oh, please.

Oh . . . . . and I am trying to
convince my mom to send me to summer
camp, the same place you are going.
(I'm pretty sure that it will work . . . .
because I think that she feels a little
guilty about my being so upset about the
move.)

Anyway, here's my notes about the
houses.

Amber Brown's Thoughts about the Search for the Perfect House!

Okay, let me begin by saying that
there is no perfect house . . . . . not
perfect for all three of us (me, Max and
Mom) . . . . . not perfect for any one of
us. . . . There were some things that
we all loved . . . . some that two of us

loved and some that only one of us loved
. . . . and some that we all hated. . . . .
All of the houses had the basics . . .
kitchens, living rooms, bedrooms, bath-
rooms.

We have narrowed it down to two
houses . . . . . that's the good news. . . .
The bad news is that one of the houses
is NOT in town . . . . . and the even
worse news is that it is wonderful . . . . .
a swimming pool in the backyard . . . . a
real in-the-ground swimming pool. There
are three stories to the house and my
bedroom would be on the third floor in a
round room that looks like the tower of a

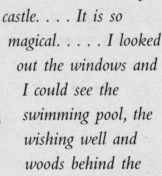

castle. . . . It is so
magical. . . . . I looked
out the windows and
I could see the
swimming pool, the
wishing well and
woods behind the

garden area. . . . . There's a fireplace in the living room and one in the kitchen. . . .

Max and Mom say that the bad news is that the house is a "fixer-upper" and would take a lot of time and money to get it all fixed up. I think that the bad news is that it is two towns away, and I would have to switch schools.

The second house is in town.

There is no swimming pool and not a lot of land.

The house is brand-new and is in "wonderful shape" (the real estate lady kept saying that). . . . . It's an okay house, but it is very boring. The one really good thing is that it is in the same new development as my friend Kelly Green (and another classmate, Hal).

Max and Mom like the first house

because it is so unique . . . . they like
the second house because it is so new, it
does not need repairs. . . . . The fireplace
in the second house does not have a
family of birds living in it. (The first
house does!) Mom thinks that the first
house is "totally charming." She likes the
second house because it has all new air
conditioners, a finished basement, a lot of
closets, all brand-new appliances. There
is even a continuous-cleaning oven. (I
personally think that it's a little strange
to have an oven that cleans itself . . . .
although I do wish that it had a
bedroom for me that cleaned itself!!)

Max and Mom say that since she is
selling our house, and he is selling his
apartment, we can afford either house. . . .
That's more of the good news. . . . The
bad news is that if we buy the wonderful
first house, there will be more money to

spend on fixing it up, and we will have to be much more careful about spending money on things like vacations.

If we buy the second house, I can stay at the same school with all of my friends. I will still be able to easily get to the place where my dad lives and I will be able to see the Marshalls as often as I do now.

If I am at the first house, I can invite everyone around here (except for my dad) to go swimming in our pool. Max did say that he would have to teach me how to help clean the pool and it would be my job to take out any frogs or skunks that fell into the pool. (I think that he is kidding . . . . . but I'm not absolutely sure about that.)

Max and Mom are not sure which house is best. . . . They are going to think about it, and they want me to think about it, and then we will talk about it. (They are afraid that someone else will bid on whichever house we decide on . . . . . so we have to decide quickly.)

That's the end of my report for now. My father is picking me up in a few minutes because he wants to talk to me about what happened last weekend. (I am so mad at him!!!!!!!!!! Is it okay for me to say that sometimes my dad acts like a real jerk???????????)

Your old friend,

Amber

Chapter
Fourteen

My father and I are sitting at the diner that
we used to go to before he moved into the
Marshall house.

He took me there so that we can have
some privacy to talk.

I am ordering. "I would like a ham and
cheese on white bread, please . . . . no tomato.
Mayo on the ham side, mustard on the cheese
side. Coleslaw in a separate dish. A Vanilla
Coke, two ice cubes."

The waitress smiles and looks at my father. "This is a girl who knows what she
wants."

I know what I want for lunch. . . . I wish
I knew where I want to live.

My father nods. "Sometimes that's good.
Sometimes it's not."

I glare at my father.

We both know that he is not talking about
my lunch order.

As for my lunch order, mayo just tastes

better on the ham side . . . . . mustard on
the cheese side . . . . . and I just like squishy
white bread . . . . . and the liquid from the
coleslaw can leak on the sandwich and make
it yucky . . . . . and too many ice cubes
change the taste of the soda . . . . . everyone knows that.

My father orders the cheeseburger deluxe
and a cup of coffee.

The waitress leaves and we just sit there,
saying nothing.

I am not going to be the one who talks
first.

He's the one who called me for this special meeting.

It's not even one of the days that we've
worked out with the custody agreement.

I don't have to be here.

I don't want to be here.

But I said yes.

Mom said that I should tell him how I
feel.

Mom said that I should tell him why I did what I did.

I just sit here thinking.

So what if I called Mom on the Sunday of the weekend that I was supposed to be with Dad.

So what if I asked her to come right over and pick me up.

It was noon, and my dad wasn't even awake yet.

He came in at about 4:00 in the morning.

I heard him talking to Brenda and Polly when he paid them for the Ambersitting.

The girls went upstairs to Polly's house.

I pretended that I was asleep when he came into the room to check on me.

In the morning, I woke up, went to the kitchen, got cereal and turned on cartoons.

My father never came out of his room.

I looked in to make sure that he was there.

He was there, snoring.

I took a shower, got dressed and waited.

He was still asleep.

At noon, I called my mother.

I was crying.

She said that she would come right over.

I packed my bags and waited for her outside in the driveway.

She was there in fifteen minutes.

I can depend on my mom.

She put my bags into the trunk, and I got into the car.

Mom said that I should write a note telling my father where I was.

I started to cry and said that I wouldn't go back in there.

She drove the car out of the driveway and parked on the street.

Sitting there, we talked about what was upsetting me.

My mom looked really angry when I told her what happened.

She took out her cell phone and called my dad and left a message on his machine saying that I was with her.

My father has been calling for several days now, but I wouldn't talk to him.

The waitress delivers our food.

I squish the bread.

"Amber," he says, "talk to me."

I glare at him and sneer.

What does he want me to say? That I think he is a jerk for making promises and not keeping them . . . . . for going on a last-minute date with a stranger when he was supposed to be with me?

I say nothing.

"You are being very immature." He frowns.

"I am immature," I finally say. "I'm nine years old . . . . what's your excuse?"

He looks furious.

I am surprised that I have just said that to him, but I am very glad . . . also a little scared.

He sounds furious. "If I had said something like that to my father, I would have been punished."

"It's the truth," I say. "I should not be punished for telling the truth."

Then I say, "How could you have gone out like that when you said that we were going to do something?"

"I have a right to my own life." He makes a face. "Do you know how much I've given up for you?"

I feel like he's hit me.

He gets quiet for a minute and then says, "I didn't mean it the way it sounded. It's

145

just that you have to understand . . . . I'm not living in New York City because I want to be closer to you. I can't socialize when you are with me."

For a minute I feel guilty, and then I think about it. "I didn't ask you to do that . . . and Mom never complains about taking care of me . . . . . and I know that there are times that she and Max are not together because of me . . . . . and they don't think I'm so much trouble. If you feel that way, just go get an apartment in New York. Just don't expect me to go there. And I don't care how much you go to court . . . . . I'll tell them I hate you!"

What happens next is something I don't expect.

My father cries.

It's very weird to see him cry.

He does it quietly, but I know that he is crying.

"Amber," he says softly, "I'm sorry that I

hurt your feelings. I love you more than anything else in the world."

I just sit there, not really believing him.

"I'm a jerk," he says.

That I do believe. "Yes, you are."

He doesn't yell. "I'll try to be better. Give me another chance. You are my daughter. I love you."

Another decision to make . . . . . do I give him another chance . . . . . do I tell him that I never want to see him again?

I'm only in the fourth grade. Why do I have to make such big decisions . . . where to live, whether to deal with my dad.

He says, "Next week . . . . please stay at the house. We'll make up a set of rules and regulations."

"Not for me," I say. "I already do what I'm supposed to."

"Like the time you got your ears pierced after you were told not to?" He smiles.

Parents remember some things too well.

I don't give in, though. "I'm not the one who has to change this time."

He sighs. "Okay. You're right."

I am feeling a little calmer now.

I'm not sure that I believe him, but I would like to.

"I promise not to be a jerk anymore," he says. "I'll try not to be a jerk."

I decide to give him one more chance.

He may be a jerk . . . but he is my jerk . . . he is my father.

Chapter
Fifteen

Dear Justin,
   I, Amber Brown, have made my decisions.
   Max and Mom and Dad have all made their decisions.
   Things are now worked out . . . . . I hope.
   Here's what's happening.
   We are buying the boring house in town. With all of the changes happening in my life, I am not sure that I want to give up all of the things that I'm used to . . . not even for a round room and a swimming pool. I will stay in my school,

keep my friends (and my enemy Hannah Burton, yuck). Mrs. Holt will still be my teacher. Mr. Robinson my principal. (We had Twizzlers and soda in his office to celebrate my decision.)

So much in my life is changing.

I want some things to stay the same.

As for my dad, he has decided to stay in New Jersey at the Marshalls' . . . and to "make some attitude adjustments." (That's what he said . . . I think he is getting some help from a counselor he has started going to for advice.) Anyway, I'm giving him another chance. He is my dad.

My mom and Max will be getting married soon. I'm going to be bridesmaid for my mom and "best man" for Max. (Only we are going to call it "best child.") I get to choose my outfit for that. (I, Amber Brown, will not wear a pink frilly dress.)

When they get married and go on
their honeymoon to Italy, I will be going
to Disneyland with Aunt Pam and
staying with her until they come back!!!!!!
Great, huh!?!!!

Your friend,

Amber

Life can be very confusing . . . . filled
with good things and filled with bad things.
But it's my life . . . . . and I have choices.

PAULA DANZIGER loves to write, and most of all, she loves to write for and about kids. She has written more than thirty books about characters who seem so real that readers really want to know them.

Amber Brown is one of these beloved characters— and she's funny, a little messy, and a very good friend.

Paula Danziger lives in Woodstock, New York; New York City; and London. And she loves pinball.

WATCH OUT, WORLD!
¡GABÍ ESTÁ AQUÍ!
(THAT MEANS: GABÍ IS HERE!)

With her friends and *familia* by her side, **GABÍ** is ready for anything... sort of. Her worst enemy, Johnny Wiley, is driving her crazy. And now **GABÍ** has to spend the whole entire month working with him on a school project!

GABÍ's so mad she keeps jumbling her English words with her Spanish words. Now she's speaking a mix of both, and no one knows *what* she's saying. Will **GABÍ** ever make sense again? Or will she be tongue-tied forever?